Crickets
on the Go

Written by Sarah Tatler
Illustrated by Al Blick

ScottForesman

A Division of HarperCollins*Publishers*

It's a sunny morning.
It's time to go.

This little cricket hops in a car.

This little cricket hops in a truck.

4

This little cricket hops on a train.

This little cricket hops on a bike.

This little cricket hops
on roller skates.

There they go,
zoom, zoom, zoom—
on their way
to their new classroom.

8